The Nanny Diaries

#4

Sierra Bottoms

Printed in the United States of America

ISBN: 9781952422140
First Printing, 2021

DarlingCoxx@gmail.com
Instagram: @DarlingCoxx
OnlyFans: @DarlingCoxx
Twitter: @DarlingCoxx

Chapter One

Dear Diary,

Adult life couldn't have begun much worse. I was set to start college with my two best friends living two states away. I had been accepted, picked out my classes, decided my extracurricular activities. Everything was ready!

Then I found out the money my parents had been saving for my college fund since I was a kid was nonexistent. They had dipped into it here and there over the years until they bled it dry. I wish they would've told me a lot sooner. I could've studied a little harder to try for better scholarships. That's what they were counting on to pay my way: scholarships. If I'd known, maybe it'd be different.

I don't want to be saddled with debt when I graduate, so I switched schools instead of taking out loans. I'm staying local, going to the junior college first then a state school which isn't nearly as expensive as where I wanted to go. I'm not mad I can't go to my chosen school. I'm mad I have to do it alone without the two girls who've been my friend since the first day of kindergarten.

And, yes, I'm mad that I have to pay for it mostly all by myself. The folks have offered to contribute a little bit each semester. It might be enough to cover the cost of my books and other supplies, but little else. I have to get a job to pay my way, and probably will only be able to afford to go part-time which means it will take twice as long to graduate. They say life doesn't go according to plan, but it would've been nice to at least make an attempt at the plan before everything fell apart.

Three days ago, I began my attempt in finding a job to pay for college. I had an interview at a deli. I figured it was easy money, and I could work around my college schedule. Mind you, I didn't want the job, not in the least. I didn't want any job at all right now. I wanted to be able to focus on school and activities, nothing else. If I had to work, food service was the last thing I wanted to do, but I didn't have much choice if I wanted flexible hours.

My first shift was today. I showed up a few minutes early and told the girl at the counter I was there to begin my training. Imagine my surprise when Aidan walked out from the back to meet me. He was the shift leader, and no, he's not working his way through college either.

Aidan is two years older than me, and he was my first boyfriend in high school. He's the type of guy who is attractive as hell, but you know you shouldn't be around because he's bad news. I fell in love with him the moment I laid eyes on him, and it took until Homecoming for him to even notice me, longer for him to ask me out.

We went steady for almost two years. We continued to date after he graduated throughout that summer, but it wasn't long before I started seeing him less and less. Shortly before my junior year, he dumped me, and I was devastated.

Then the asshole came crawling back a couple months later talking about how he couldn't live without me. It was too late. I was seeing someone new. I realized he's not right for me, not boyfriend material for anyone if I'm being honest. That doesn't mean the sex isn't unbelievable. My friends have this theory it's because he was my first. Maybe they're right. It's like my body recognizes his scent.

I hadn't been old enough to date yet, so my parents didn't know about him. I'd leave to head over to a friend's house and wait down the street for him to pick me up. That's how we did it the whole time we were together. Well, until the last few months of our relationship anyway. Once I turned sixteen we didn't have to sneak around anymore.

We'd find a place to park and sit for the night. There was no way I would risk going on an actual date with him because if someone saw us who knew my folks, that'd be the end of me. The name Sierra Bottoms would be in the obituary if my father even suspected there had been a boy in my life.

I didn't mind. Sometimes we hung out with friends, but we'd usually take time to ourselves before the night was over. Even before he popped my cherry, we'd have alone time to talk or make out.

The night we first had sex was quite an experience. I was very naïve and innocent. I mean I knew the basics, but I really didn't know anything about it at all if I'm being honest. Looking back, I'm glad Aidan had been able to figure it out. I had hoped he wouldn't that night going into it, but if he hadn't, he probably would've just thought I was a terrible lay.

I couldn't tell Aidan I was a virgin. He was a bad boy like I said which meant he had no intention of doing right by me or being faithful. Don't get me started on the number of times he cheated on me. He wasn't completely bad. I know he would've never fucked me if he knew I was a virgin.

We hadn't been dating long and had only made out a few times. Usually by the time we left our friends and had time to ourselves, it was close to when I needed to be home. One night, he decided to cut out our friends altogether and drove straight to one of our favorite parking spots. I knew what was coming, or rather, it was one of the many possibilities that went through my mind. I might have been naïve, but I wasn't stupid.

To be honest, I don't think I was ready. He didn't pressure me. He didn't have to. I gave myself to him willingly. Don't get me wrong. It's not that I didn't want him. I did. I wanted him to be my first too. But if he was anyone else, I don't think I would've lost my virginity my freshman year. I thought he'd dump me if I said no. It was my own fears and insecurities, nothing he said or did. I didn't want to lose him, so I gave myself to him sooner than I had planned. That's how I see it.

As far as my sexual history goes, it was the worst time I ever had, but it was also my best in a way. Aidan had pulled off the country road and turned onto an access road through a corn field on his granddad's property. It was one of a handful of places we usually went to make out or sneak a few beers. It surprised me we were headed there so early that night, but like I said, I was young and ignorant. I thought maybe he already knew no one was out and about to hang out with.

The corn had already been harvested, so Aidan's truck would be visible from the road. Cars rarely traveled that part of the country around town unless they lived in those parts. The weather was perfect for as late in the season as it was. It was one of those years where autumn stayed warmed, holding onto summer as long as it could.

Aidan put the truck in park, rolled down the windows, and then killed the engine. We talked for a few minutes. I don't remember about what. I remember not being nervous, not knowing what was coming, and feeling like I was right where I belonged.

He leaned over and kissed me for a couple minutes and played with my breasts. It was something I'd let him do before. Making out was something we typically did at the end of the evening, not at the beginning. I still hadn't put two and two together definitively. He slid his hand down over my abdomen, in between my legs, and rubbed over the top of my jeans. It felt good. We had just moved to third base for the first time.

I knew our progress was going along kind of fast, but I still didn't think it would be anything more that night until he unbuttoned my jeans. I put my hand down to stop him. He sat up straight in the cab, and asked, "So you don't want to then?"

That's when everything came crashing in like a tidal wave. It all clicked. He wasn't after some petty make out session. He wanted it all.

He didn't ask if I was ready. He didn't say sorry for moving too fast. Nothing. It was simply, *'So you don't want to then?'*

He didn't say it angrily. Even looking back now, I can't remember anything about his actions or words that made me think he was upset I pushed his hand away. Somehow I still felt like it was now or never. I wanted to continue to be his girlfriend, and I wanted him to eventually be my first. I would've just liked to have waited a little bit longer. I didn't know what to say, and I was afraid of telling him the truth. I glanced around nervously, trying to find the words.

He leaned in and said, "Its okay. Even if someone drives by, no one will see what we're doing in here."

Aidan thought I was just worried about getting caught when in reality, I was worried about so many things, but getting caught hadn't crossed my mind. I leaned in to kiss him and let him do the rest. He immediately went for my pants again, unbuttoning them, taking my kiss as an open invitation.

Within a few minutes, it was over. I moved to sit up as quickly as possible. I worried I had bled all over the bench of his truck. I sorted through my clothes, getting dressed as quickly as possible. It took Aidan all of fifteen seconds to fix up his pants. It's a little unfair how much a woman has to take off compared to a man to be able to do anything.

When I was completely dressed except for my shoes, he reached his arm out to me to come to him. I slid across the seat and melted into his arms. The pain was mostly gone, but there was still a little raw, residual ache. I knew I would heal soon enough. For now, it was a reminder of what I had done.

He put his arm around me, pulling me tight. "Why didn't you tell me you were a virgin?" he asked.

I was mortified. I never thought he would be able to figure it out.

"Huh? Why didn't you?" he asked again when I didn't answer.

"I didn't think you would sleep with me if you knew," I told him honestly. It was a half-truth, but it was the truth nonetheless.

He didn't say anything in response which in my mind always cemented it as fact that I had been right.

Chapter Two

Dear Diary,

Today was my fifth shift at the deli, and my second shift out of training. It's also the day I got fired from my first job.

Yesterday was my first day not having someone breathing over my shoulder, judging my every move. I think it went pretty well. I had to ask a couple questions, but other than that, everything went smoothly. The only problem was I worked with Aidan for the first time since I started.

It wasn't really a problem to work with him. He's good at his job and was quite professional when it came to working with an ex-girlfriend. The real problem was the attraction between us.

Honestly, I hadn't much thought about him since soon after we broke up right before my junior year. It hurt, of course. He had been my first everything. My first love, my first sex, and even my first kiss were all memories tied to him. Within a couple months, he graduated, and I found a new boyfriend. There really wasn't much looking back after that. Out of sight, out of mind as they say.

Being around him again, my body reacted wildly. It was like somehow I recognized him on a physical level. As the shift went on, we spent more time side by side or in some near vicinity. With each passing minute, I became more and more wet. I wanted him with a passion I'd never experienced.

It had to be one sided. There was no hint from him whatsoever that he had a similar reaction. Not only that, but there was no indication that he noticed how I reacted to him. Every time he came near, my breath caught, and my pulse quickened. Aidan was oblivious to it all.

At the end of our shift, we had to do the closing duties. The deli was closed, and the doors were locked. Aidan, as shift manager, handled the money while I cleaned up in the front. We had stayed on top of dishes during the evening, so there were very few waiting on us. He took care of them when he finished the deposit.

All that was left was the prep work for the morning. We had a list of what needed to be moved from the freezer, and there were some items from the stock room that needed to be replenished. I was in there grabbing a couple boxes of things we needed when I heard him come into the room. I figured he was through with the dishes and came to help with the last of the work, so we could get out of there sooner.

As I reached for a box of napkins, he came up behind me, putting his hand on a shelf of the storage rack above me and leaned in next to me. "I've been lusting for five minutes alone with you all night," he breathed heavily into my ear.

I moaned. His soft words, his breath, the closeness, all of it made my knees weak. I'd been lusting after him just as much.

His lips softly grazed the nape of my neck, and I almost buckled. The two boxes I was holding dropped from my hands and fell to the floor. I leaned back into him, and he wrapped his arms around me. His mouth explored my neck and shoulders while his hands traveled my body. He gently squeezed my breasts and rubbed my crotch through the slacks that was required as part of the uniform.

"I didn't think I'd ever get you alone," he whispered in my ear.

Apparently, I wasn't the only one affected by this sudden reunion. I could feel his stiff bulge press against me and knew he'd been wanting this the whole shift.

Aidan unfastened my pants and stuck his hand inside. He slid his hand down between my legs and teased my pussy before rubbing my clit. I arched my back and pressed my ass against him.

He was no good for me in a relationship, no good for any woman really. He was a controlling, jealous jerk with most of the women he'd been with, but I probably had the nicest version of him. I didn't want anything more from him than physical satisfaction in that moment. I wanted sex, plain and simple. I wanted him to fuck me in the back room of the deli amid the boxes of napkins, plastic silverware, and individual packets of condiments. And, I would hand those items out to customers during each shift from that moment forward relishing in the faint smell of sex that lingered on them.

He spun me around to face him and laid a big kiss on my lips. Quickly, his mouth traveled south to my neck as he fumbled with untucking my shirt. I pushed his hands away to do it myself. There was no need for seduction or persuasion. This was going to happen, and it needed to happen fast.

In minutes, I was naked, and he had his shirt off with his pants around his ankles. He lifted me to rest my ass on a shelf, but the wired metal cut into my flesh, and I pushed him back. This wasn't going to work.

Aidan looked around for an alternate location. Instead, he picked up his shirt and put it on the shelf to soften my seat a little. It didn't help much, but it did enough. I put my face on a large box on the floor in front of the shelves to brace myself. He inched himself between my legs while laying on all the lines of how much he missed me.

"I never forgot about you."

"I've wanted this since the moment you came in for your first shift."

"You were the one who got away."

"Damn, I've missed you so much."

I finally had to tell him to shut his mouth and fuck me. This was a sure thing. He didn't have to bait me into it, and I knew every word that fell from his lips was bullshit.

Aidan guided the tip of his cock inside my labyrinth then positioned himself. He grabbed my hips and began thrusting into me. It felt amazing. He wasn't the best fuck

I've ever had, but there was something about our chemistry that gave it something extra.

I held the side brace of the shelving unit with one hand and rested my other on his shoulder. The precarious position I was in made it difficult to do much without worrying about falling or toppling the shelves. I bucked into him the best I could, and tightened the walls of my pussy to massage his sweet dick each time he entered me.

The deli was closed, and the doors were locked. I didn't worry about staying quiet. I moaned loudly without a care. Aidan began thrusting harder, responding to the sounds of my pleasure.

My first orgasm came quick. It was my body's gratitude for getting the cock it had lusted for all day. The second one took more effort with how uncomfortable it was sitting on the metal shelves.

"Fuck me," I demanded. "Harder. Own me."

Aidan didn't hesitate. He pounded into me and teased my tits with his teeth. I took my hand off his shoulder and squeezed it between our sweaty bodies to play with my clit. My second orgasm came quick after that.

Midway through my ecstasy, I realized Aidan was getting close. I only hoped I finished first. Having a man pull out at that moment is agony. Then he started bucking and grunting while inside me.

"Asshole!" I cried out, pushing him back. "You're damn lucky I'm on birth control."

The jerk just smiled at me. What a douche. I was pissed at him, but my anger was quickly lost as I looked around. There were a couple crashes while we were fucking, but by the looks of the floor, half the supplies on the shelves had fallen from the steady jolting against the shelves during our sex. It was a huge mess.

I giggled. It just came out, and I didn't attempt to stop it. Aidan turned to see what I was looking at, and he laughed. He pulled his pants up, and turned to me. "Get dressed. Looks like we created more work for ourselves," he said, still smiling.

Most of it was picked up when I finished tucking in my shirt. I took my own sweet time. The fact that he didn't pull out when he came was still weighing on me. This would definitely be the only hook up between us after that, and I saw him being shouldered with most of my side work every shift we worked together until I got over it. That would be never.

We finally finished everything up and went home, separately. When I came back today for my next shift, I was immediately asked to step into the managers' office. I wasn't worried about anything being wrong. I knew I was doing a good job. I figured it was routine, checking on availability, or reviewing how I was doing on my own which I already knew was good.

I was not expecting to be told, "It bewilders me that I even have to tell an employee sex is not allowed on the premises even if it's after the deli closes. We serve food here. I shouldn't have to tell you how the health department would feel about it."

'That fucking asshole,' I thought. It wouldn't make sense for him to tell the boss since he'd get into trouble as well, but he probably told all the other employees about his conquests. Someone leaked it to management

which meant I had to sit through this humiliating meeting where I'd promise it was a moment of weakness. I'd lie that we only kissed, and it wouldn't happen again.

I didn't get the chance. The manager turned the laptop to face me. Apparently there are cameras in the store room. Who knew? On the screen were several security camera images, and one of them showed us at the beginning, still fully dressed, with my ass pressed against Aidan.

Shit! I had no idea there was a camera in that room! It wasn't an easily visible one that's for sure. We were beyond busted. We couldn't even lie and claim it was a nasty rumor that had little basis in truth.

Anyway, that's how I came to be fired from my new job before I barely had a chance to work it.

Chapter Three

Dear Diary,

I barely got the job at the insurance agency. Well, I wouldn't exactly say barely. I was severely under qualified. Plus the ad for the job said part-time, flexible hours. When I interviewed, Mr. Scott told me the position was from 8am-1pm, Monday through Friday. I don't see anything about that to indicate flexibility in the hours.

My current college classes are in the morning three days a week and in the afternoon on the other two. In fact, those classes start at 1pm, so I wouldn't be available for the shift on any day. It was frustrating being there in the interview because I felt like it was a waste of my time. If the ad for the job had been more forthcoming, I'd never have applied.

During the interview, I noticed Mr. Scott's eyes rarely met mine. He seemed to focus solely on the area below my neck. I wore a nice button top with a black skirt, trying to look professional. The top was a little tight as I usually didn't have to dress up like this, and the material pulled apart around the buttons over my breasts.

I chose to take advantage of his interest. Don't judge me. It's not like I'm the first woman to ever use her assets to get what she wanted, or needed in my case. When he shuffled around the papers on his desk including my resume, application and the interview questionnaire, I quickly undid the top button. Well, the top button I had fastened anyway. It exposed my cleavage, and I moved around in my chair to lean forward a bit to show it off even more.

It worked. When he looked my way again, his mouth fell open for several seconds. He stuttered when he began speaking. "Wh-where w-were we?" he asked. "Oh, yeah. Work h-h-history."

"I know I don't have much experience in an office setting," I told him.

He looked at me then glanced

around the room before looking at the papers in front of him again. "You don't have much work experience at all, Sierra." he corrected.

"Call me Skitts. Like Skittles," I said. It was a childhood nickname I hated, but I needed him to think of me as a sweet treat he could put in his mouth. "I realize that. My parents always put the focus on my studies and wouldn't allow me to work, but now I need to pay for college."

This job had to happen for me. Interviews were few and far between even though everyone claimed to be hiring. The two credit cards I applied for at the start of the semester were already almost maxed. One was, and the other was on its way. If I didn't get an income soon, I wouldn't be able to continue making my tuition payments.

It was a damn catch twenty-two. My parents made too much money for me to be eligible for any assistance except scholarships. I wasn't granted any of the ones I applied for either. On the other hand, their bills were too high compared to their income to really be able to help pay for my schooling. The last thing I wanted to do was take out student loans.

I figured I could go to a junior college and get an associates degree which might help me find a better paying job. That way I could afford to work toward my bachelors. I was going to be done after the first semester if something didn't go my way soon.

"I'm a fast learner though," I told him, not sure how I could prove it having only four work shifts under my belt for my entire life. "Besides, I grew up on a computer."

Mr. Scott nodded slowly. "Your generation does tend to have a better grasp on electronics and software than mine does."

I wondered how old he was. There were pictures on his desk of two children around the ages of eight and ten if I had to guess. No pictures of their mother were anywhere in sight, and he didn't wear a wedding band.

I managed to get the job after all. I'd like to say it was because of some skill, but I know it was my cleavage that got me hired. Mr. Scott is allowing me to work around my classes this semester. I'm doing two mornings and three afternoons a week at the office. The catch is that in the spring, I have to take all my classes in the afternoon, evenings or online to be able to work the 8am-1pm hours like he wants.

Today was my third day on the job, and I still feel like an imposter. The filing, faxing, making copies, and creating folders for new clients are all things I can do in my sleep. Every phone call is another question that I don't know how to answer. I have to patch it through to Mr. Scott, or take a number to call back if he's busy. He assures me I will pick it up in time. It still makes me feel like I'm not doing a good job.

If that's not enough, the software he uses is becoming my arch nemesis. I follow my notes exactly. Someone will call to schedule an appointment as a new customer for example. I go into the system, put in all their information, and select the type of appointment from the drop down, so it schedules the right amount of time. I save it all, but when I go back to check, something is wrong. The client's information didn't save. Or the appointment type is wrong. I don't know what it is I'm doing to mess it up.

Luckily, I realized early on I wasn't capable of mastering the software. I right everything on a notepad, attempt to enter it myself, but when I fail miserably, I have all the necessary information for Mr. Scott to fix it. He puts it in exactly the way I did the first time, and it works! I'm starting to think the computer just hates me.

It's not just scheduling either. I'll open the file to print signature forms for added fire insurance. It will print earthquake. I've been using electronics since damn near before I could talk, but somehow this computer evades me.

Mr. Scott keeps trying to

reassure me. "You're new."

"You'll get it."

"It takes time."

"Rome wasn't built in a day."

I appreciate the support, but I can't help but feel like my days are numbered. My one and only job before this only lasted four shifts, and my fourth shift here is tomorrow.

Regardless of what he says, I know what's really saving me is his lust for me. Whenever we talk, he's staring at my chest. I've caught him checking out my ass numerous times a day. When he's helping me on the computer, he leans in close enough that I can feel his breath on my neck. I know he's staring down my shirt.

I've been using it to my advantage. I always wear a button up with an extra button or two undone. Once a customer pulls up in the small lot out front, I fix my shirt to display a more professional appearance. When it's just Mr. Scott and I in the office, I show off all I can without it being considered indecent exposure.

It's a funny thing to flirt like this and use your body to your advantage to get what you want. Mr. Scott isn't exactly what I'd consider attractive. I'm sure he is quite a catch to any middle aged single lady out there. I'm barely out of high school! I don't want an old man breathing down my neck, and I've never looked twice at one before now.

Since I started playing with him like this, that's changed. It's actually turning me on seeing how he reacts whenever he looks at me. The way he inhales suddenly, licks his lips, half growls as he swallows down whatever explicit emotion that's raging through his body, or turns quickly to block the view of his groin when the effect on him becomes physical.

I enjoy his reactions, and it stirs the heat between my legs. I'm usually wet as fuck by the time I clock out. I've found myself wondering what his body looks like beneath that suit he wears every day. I imagine he's slightly athletic with a hairy chest and solid build.

It still astonishes me even as I write these words, but I want him to make a move. I want him to take things from this massive office tension that's built between us and lay it out bare for us to enjoy. I want Mr. Scott to fuck me.

Chapter Four

Dear Diary,

I worked for Mr. Scott for three weeks. It had been rather good. I earned enough to make my next tuition payment and pay a little on one of my credit cards. If I had managed to keep the job, I would've been able to continue making my tuition payments for the rest of the semester as well as paid off that card.

It started as me not so innocently wanting to make sure he'd keep me around even if I couldn't master all of my job duties. It took about a week, but I finally figured out the computer system. I'm still not sure what I had been doing wrong at first. All of a sudden, things changed. I started doing everything right.

I continued to play into his lust, wearing clothing that would allow him to ogle me easier. It was amusing until it wasn't. I began to realize he was a good looking man even if he was close to twice my age. The way he stared at me, undressing me with his eyes, began to turn me on. It seeped over to my evenings at home. I had fantasies about him and touching myself to the thought of going down on him while he sat in the big leather chair behind his desk.

It wouldn't take much. That

was obvious. All I had to do was let him know I was just as into him as he was into me. He would have his way with me right then I was sure.

I just really needed this job. I needed to pay for college. I wasn't sure about mixing business with pleasure. Then today it all came to a head.

The last I got laid was with Aidan in the backroom of the deli. I have needs too. I know us girls aren't supposed to, but we do.

It was looking like my plan backfired a little. I'd spent every day growing the tension between us intentionally. I figured the more he wanted to fuck my brains out the less likely he'd fire me over being slow to get the hang of things in the office. The problem was that now I needed him to fuck the hell out of me. If he didn't make a move soon, I was going to have to risk everything and make it myself.

It's true what they say. Be careful what you wish for.

It was Friday afternoon, and it was a miserably wet day. The rain was relentless. My white blouse got a little wet between the car and the office door, and it may have been on purpose. I'll never tell.

The afternoon was dead which meant there was plenty of free time for Mr. Scott to get an eye full whenever he wanted. He spent the better part of two hours working alongside me, making sure I had caught on to everything, and that the front end workload was caught up.

What happened next was straight out of a cheesy cable channel romance movie. Our hands brushed, and we nervously smiled then looked away. When it happened again, our eyes locked, and he leaned in for a kiss. It was short lived before he broke away, apologizing profusely and swearing it would never happen again.

Well, I couldn't have that. While he was swearing on everything that was holy it was an accident, I grabbed the sides of his head with my hands and laid one on him. Mr. Scott never protested.

We were all over each other in the reception area. We turned round and round leaning against the desk, the file cabinets, even the customer chairs. There was a big picture window facing the parking lot and beyond that, the street. Anyone who dared to brave the weather and happened to be driving by would have quite a sight to behold.

Mr. Scott wanted a bit more privacy than that. He pulled away and motioned for me to wait. He locked the front door, putting the close sign in place. Then he went to my desk, and it looked like he was making a call. He must've noticed the weird look on my face because he explained what he was doing.

"Transferring the calls to the after-hours number a little early," he said smiling.

Once he was done, he grabbed my hands and gently lifted me from the chair I had collapsed into. He pulled me into his arms and smothered me with his mouth as he walked me backward down the hall to his office doorway.

When we were safely inside his office and out of view of anyone passing by, Mr. Scott changed from mild mannered insurance salesman to ravaging sex machine. I wasn't exactly the same naïve, inexperienced little girl I was that night in Aidan's pickup parked in the middle of a field. I wasn't a massive slut either, but I had learned a thing or two about what to do during sex and how to please a man. All of that seemed like child's play compared to being with Mr. Scott. He put my skill and know how to shame with every touch of his fingertips.

His fingers were like magic on my body. With every touch, I learned what I had been missing out on with the boys in my life. He was a professional, and they were merely amateurs.

Mr. Scott's mouth gently caressed my neck and bosom. His lips and tongue guided me to heights I had never reached from attention solely above the waist. Within minutes, I had a want, better yet a need to feel him inside me like I had never experienced.

"Oh, Sierra," he moaned. "Are

you sure?"

"Yes!" I cried out a little too excitedly. "I want you. I need to feel you."

He reached under my skirt and removed my panties. "I've wanted this since the day you first walked in this door."

I smiled. I knew I had him at the interview. It took me longer to realize I wanted him too.

"We don't have much time," he said softly. His voice sounded regretful. "I can't keep the door locked like that."

"That's fine," I told him.

He didn't seem to want to accept my agreement for a quickie. For a moment, I worried he'd change his mind about fucking me altogether.

"There's always next time to do it right, but you can't deny me now," I said. I grabbed his bulge through his slacks and began stroking it.

Mr. Scott stared deeply into my eyes, burning into my soul. "Oh, fuck, Sierra. I can't wait."

With one hand, he swiped his planner and other accessories off his desk and laid me on my back with the other. I yelled out in excitement. This is exactly what I'd been fantasizing about day after day while trying to concentrate on my work. I shimmied around into a better position while he undid his pants, letting them drop to his ankles.

He reached under my skirt and toyed with my pussy lips and clit briefly before I felt the head of his knob press against my entrance. I hadn't even been able to get a good look at him, but judging by the quick feel I got, he was a bit bigger than average.

Mr. Scott leaned forward, and my labyrinth gave way to his stiff shaft.

"Ohhhh," I moaned. It felt amazing to finally have this fulfillment after weeks of constant teasing.

"Damn, Sierra," he grunted, shifting around to find a better position. He began thrusting into me long and slow, following the sounds of my moans as if they were directing him. The louder and longer I groaned the harder and faster he fucked me.

"I'm almost there," I muttered. "Oh! Fuck! Me!"

He rubbed my clit with his thumb while driving his cock deep inside me.

My pussy convulsed and tightened around his pulsating member as my cum juices flowed onto him and the mahogany under my ass. He continued to thrust into me, keeping steady time, allowing me to ride out my orgasm longer.

When my climax was over, he leaned atop me for a quick kiss then lifted one of my legs over his shoulder. He grabbed my hips and bucked into me forcefully.

"Douglass!" a woman's voice called out from somewhere close by.

I froze, but Mr. Scott's eyes widened in fear. He pulled out and zipped his pants before turning in the direction of the very angry woman standing in the doorway.

"Lisa," he muttered nervously. "You're early."

I didn't move much except to close my legs and make sure my skirt was pulled down. I could see enough to watch her strain her neck around to look at me laying across the desk behind him.

"For fucks sake, Doug!" she cried out. "How old is she?"

"Old enough," he answered, walking out of the office and taking the very angry woman with him as he went.

Their voices echoed in the hall until I heard the bell ring on the outer door. *'The door,'* I thought. *'It was locked. How hadn't we heard the bell before?'*

She had to be his wife, or girlfriend at any rate. How else would she have a key? I straightened my clothes and slid my shoes on with tears stinging the corners of my eyes. I never asked if he was single. I just assumed he was because he didn't wear a ring. That doesn't mean shit, and I know it. This was just as much my fault as it was his.

I hadn't overheard much before they went outside. Something

about she'd been trying to call both the office and his cell phone, but couldn't get through on either line. Something may have been said about kids, but I figured it was another jab at my age again. Boy was I ever wrong.

I stayed in the office until Mr. Scott came back. It was probably a ten minute wait, but it felt like an eternity. I sat there suffering in anxiety and boredom. There was no way I was going out there to face the wrath of a woman scorned.

When he sulked back inside, he looked like he had aged ten years while he was gone. He sunk into his desk with his face buried in his hands. I wondered if he even realized I was still there.

"Sierra," he finally muttered. "I'm really sorry."

"Me too," I said. My voice a little more indignant than I meant it to be. I had some of the blame, but this fuck wad knew he wasn't single when he stuck his dick in me.

"That was my ex-wife," he began.

Mr. Scott went on to explain that while the divorce was final, custody wasn't settled yet. He was supposed to have his kids this weekend and was going to pick them up after work. Lisa had to leave earlier than they had planned and wanted to drop them at the office. It wasn't uncommon for his kids to come here during business hours.

When she couldn't get ahold of him, she assumed the storms had taken out the phones. She went ahead and came by.

"I forgot she still had a key to the place. Well, I guess I didn't forget," he admitted. "I just didn't think about it earlier."

She let herself and the kids inside, and all three of them saw what was transpiring on his desk. Because of that, she wasn't letting him have his children again until after the next court date which was almost two months out.

"I'm sorry, but I'm going to have to let you go. I know it's unfair to you, but it's the best thing for me in this situation."

I stood up and headed to the door wondering if there was some lawsuit I could file over this. Yeah, there were other circumstances involved, but the fact remained that he was firing me for sleeping with him.

"I'm going to add a week's severance to your last check. It should help while you look for another job. I'm sure it won't take you long," he said to my back as I left.

Chapter Five

Dear Diary,

It took a month, but I finally found a job at Rossi's Garage. Its three afternoons a week staying into the evening hours. I was given the job on the condition that next semester I'd have three full days a week available during regular business hours. It didn't matter which three days, and I have to work every Saturday morning as well.

On each day I work into the evening, one of the mechanics has to stay with me. They take turns being the one stuck working late.

The owner doesn't trust me enough yet to leave me alone after hours which I completely understand. By the time he does, my school schedule will have changed, and I won't be here in the evenings any longer.

It's an easy job. There's some paperwork, filing, payment processing. I call people about their vehicles. I can't complain too much.

The guys didn't mind staying late even though the owner of the garage made it out to be like a huge inconvenience for them. They were being paid and continuing to work on whatever cars were in the shop. None of them seemed to mind the extra pocket money they were earning from the late hours. The only person it really seemed to bother was the owner.

My only training was Monday afternoon during the shop's hours before the owner went home. I was left to work on filing and reorganizing the office. It hadn't seen a woman's touch for a very long time. On the second day, he supervised me a little bit before deciding I was capable of handling things on my own.

It's now Friday. Tonight's mechanic chaperone was Johnny. Rossi had introduced him as his son. It didn't necessarily mean Johnny was off limits, but it did place Johnny in a danger zone. If I fuck around with the owner's son and things don't work out, it's a no brainer which of us would find ourselves without a job. It was just my luck that he was related to the owner. Johnny was the only one of the mechanics who looked good enough to eat.

I should've learned my lesson about bringing sex into the work place, but maybe I'm just a slow learner. Maybe I didn't have designs to act on anything at all. I think it's natural when you're single, and you meet someone new. You size them up and put them into neat little categories until you learn something about them that warrants a transfer. For a lot of people, the categories are friendship and dating. For me, the categories are fuckable and ew, gross.

Johnny was the only guy here in the fuckable category. There had never been so much as a look out of place from him. Then working after hours tonight, he was even more professional. He only came into the office twice. The first time was after the shop closed to let me know he'd be working in the last bay if I needed anything. He came in again a few hours later to let me know he was finished, and he wanted an idea of how much longer I'd be. He went back to clean up in the shop and said to let him know when I was ready. He was polite, friendly, and a big change from what I was used to.

The other two nights I had worked late Chris and Zak couldn't stay out of the office if their lives depended on it. They were always in there under the pretense of checking to see if I needed anything while getting their fill of me with their eyes and standing a little too close for comfort.

When I finished, I closed up the main office. I put everything away, shut down the computer, turned off the lights and went into the shop, locking the office door behind me. The main entrance had already been locked up, and the alarm system was by the shop door. It was all I could do to help Johnny out and get us out of there quicker.

I looked around, but I didn't see

Johnny. Most of the lights were off, but there was enough to see by. I went through the doorway in the back. It opened into a small hallway.

On the far left was a breakroom that I didn't use. I ate at the desk out front. No one had said anything to me about it, and I hoped they never would. The breakroom was coated in layers of grease and dirt. If I had to take my breaks in there, it would be pointless to bring food. The smell inside that room alone caused me to lose my appetite.

Next to it was an employee bathroom which I also never went into. The one for customers was in the office, and that's the one I used. It was suggested by Mr. Rossi that

I use the one near me instead of making the walk all the way back to the other one. I had a feeling it looked worse than the breakroom, and that was the real reason I got special treatment.

The light to the breakroom was off, but I opened the door anyway. The motion activated lights came on automatically. The room was empty. I knocked on the bathroom door. There was no response. I tried the knob, and it was unlocked. I slowly pushed the door hesitantly saying Johnny's name. Nothing. I continued to push it open until I could see it was empty as well.

On the other end of the hallway was Rossi's office. It was the only place I hadn't checked, and the only place he could be unless Johnny had left even just to get some air without telling me. I tried the office door, and it was unlocked. I looked around. It was a relatively small room filled with filing cabinets. There was enough room for a desk and chair as well as an old worn out couch along one wall that the owner used to nap on during the day. He kept it no secret what he was doing in his office.

The light in the office was on when I opened the door which made me hopeful, but as I looked around, I didn't see Johnny anywhere. I said his name a couple more times then stepped into the room.

The office door slammed shut

behind me. I jumped and turned around. Johnny was standing there with his back against the door. I put my hand across my chest. "You scared the hell out of me," I told him.

"I'm so sorry," he said with a sly grin. "How can I ever make it up to you?" he asked. As he spoke, he cut the distance between us with a seedy look in his eyes that made my heart beat rapidly.

He reached out to touch my upper arm where my bra strap had slid down from under the sleeveless top I was wearing. He hooked his finger in it and slowly moved it back until it was in place.

I sucked in my breath at his touch. I knew I was risking my job, my income, my ability to pay for college. I was either too young and stupid, or just too damn horny to care. I put my hands on his waist and pulled him closer.

It didn't take long until we were naked on the couch. He took his time. It was so much sweeter than my previous work trysts that had to be fast, awkward and interrupted. Johnny didn't have much to say in the way of sweet talk, but what he did with his mouth was far more amazing.

He had his head planted firmly between my legs for the longest time. I came over and over again. With one knee bent up on the couch and the other foot firmly planted on the floor, I fucked his face and grinded my pussy into his mouth. His tongue brought me to climax repeatedly, and this was the only way I could show my gratitude in this position.

After an eternity of ecstasy, he moved away from me, licking his lips and smiling. "Like that, huh?"

"Oh yeah," I said, trying to pull him on top of me.

"Not yet, Sierra baby," he said softly. Johnny swung my legs over the edge of the couch and sat next to me. He stroked his erect cock and nodded my way. "Your turn," he said. He put his hand on my shoulder and gently pushed me in the direction of his dick.

I rose up on all fours and leaned over his shaft. I took the tip in my mouth, sucking on it till I heard him moan. I lubed up his shaft with my tongue quickly then lowered my mouth on him. I took him in slowly. Each time I lowered my head, I let a little more of his member slip between my lips while working the lower part of his shaft with one hand.

I knew I could deep throat him, but that talent was reserved for more than taboo affairs with coworkers. With my other hand, I massaged his balls. As he grew closer, I took his balls into my mouth, gently sucking and toying them with my tongue before going back to his cock.

When he was about to cum, he put both hands on my head and

held me in place. He made sure I couldn't move back to avoid him shooting his load in my mouth, not that I would've tried. I swallowed every drop and continued to suck him, hoping for more.

"Damn girl," he said, leaning back into the couch. "I hope you have to work late for a long time."

Chapter Six

Dear Diary,

True to a typical asshole, Johnny bragged to the whole shop about what happened between us. I was humiliated at first till I realized it backfired on him. No one believed him, and I mean no one. Not even his best buds on the crew bought a word of it. Whenever something was said around me, I just laughed and didn't give a direct answer. All of us women learn how to deflect at a young age.

I don't think Mr. Rossi heard any of the gossip. If he did, he was a decent enough man to not let on about it in front of me. It didn't stop me from feeling anxious around him every time he stepped into the office.

By the time Friday came along, the teasing was making its way to me. Again, no one believed him for a minute, but it was his night to stay late with me. The other guys in the shop were giving me shit asking if I needed protection from Johnny that night. They were all offering to hang around to make sure I stayed safe.

It was getting old, and I let them know it. A joke is a joke, but don't drag it out until it's dead. Then it's just annoying, and it pisses me off. Haha! You're so funny. Now, shut up and get back to work because that's what I'm trying to do. I just want to get my stuff done in peace, so I can go home like everyone else.

Oh, I almost forgot. It was payday! Yay! I needed this so much. I was running out of gas to get to my classes. And don't even get me started on my tuition payments. The interest they tack on to divide up the cost is ridiculous. I would love to work a job long enough to have the next semester's payment in full. It'd save a lot of money. It was looking like it was too late to get it together for my spring classes. I could definitely do it by summer, but I wasn't sure if I was taking that semester off yet or not. But fall? Oh, yeah. As long as I stayed working, there would be no unnecessary interest paid then. The trick is keeping a job. That is the main skill I seem to lack.

Anyway, I digress. The shop closed on Friday evening. Mr. Rossi stopped by and told me to have a good weekend. He never came in on Saturday's. The mechanics began heading out one by one. They brought any paperwork and keys up to me on their way. One thing is for certain. I'd never get out of here on time even working full shifts because I have a lot to tidy up after they turn in their work orders.

It took me longer than it should have, but eventually I figured out that Chris hadn't come to the office. Johnny hadn't either, but he was stuck working until I was done.

Chris should've turned his work in by five.

I went into the shop looking for him. For all I knew he had decided to stay late to finish up a car. It was possible that's what was going on, and it hadn't been mentioned to me.

He was nowhere to be seen. I almost went right back into the office figuring he had slipped out without turning in anything. I'd get it in the morning. It wouldn't make much difference except to make sure I'd leave a few minutes early tonight because I didn't have his work to process.

I *almost* went into the office. Then I noticed Johnny was nowhere to be found either.

'Great,' I thought. *'I have to babysit a couple idiot guys acting like teenagers.'*

I went outside and walked around the back of the building thinking they probably stepped out to get high. No one had ever said anything to me directly about the amount of pot they smoked during the day, but it would take an idiot to not be able to smell it.

They weren't outside either. I went back in and headed to the door in the back of the shop. I checked the break room and the bathroom. Both were empty. I looked toward Mr. Rossi's office. The light was off. I couldn't see any light shining under the door anyway. I figured that's where they were, but I wasn't going in there. Not after what happened last week. I wouldn't mind another round with Johnny, but if this was all a set up for Chris to see if Johnny was telling the truth, I wasn't going to play.

I went back into the shop and headed to the office. They'd show up eventually. I was growing irritated. I had already hit a point where I hoped they didn't return from wherever they snuck off to by the time I was done. It'd give me the opportunity to call Mr. Rossi at home telling him I was ready to leave, but couldn't. It'd serve Johnny right for having a large fucking mouth, and Chris would have to be collateral damage.

I never made it to my computer. As I passed the van that sat in Chris' bay, an arm reached out from the open side door and grabbed me. I jumped and screamed. I almost fell backward and nearly landed on my ass.

Chris emerged from the van laughing so hard he couldn't breathe.

"Very funny, asshole," I spat.

He continued to wheeze and gag until he finally muttered, "Don't be like that. Come join the party."

I narrowed my eyes at him wondering what he meant. There was movement behind him, and I stood on my tip toes to peer over his shoulder. Johnny was sitting in the van taking a swig out of a whiskey bottle.

"C'mon in," he said, patting the seat next to him.

I knew where this was headed, and I knew it wasn't going to end well. I climbed into the van anyway.

It started out like a party as they said. We had a little bit to drink and a little more to smoke. We talked and laughed and were having a great time.

Then Chris put his hand on my leg. I shot Johnny a look. It was unclear how much of this was his direct doing. He might not have invited Chris to an after-hours threesome outright, but I still blamed him. If he'd kept his mouth shut, we wouldn't be here right now. We'd be getting our work done and possibly having a round two later on before we left. Instead, I was going to have to shut this down as quickly as possible.

Before I could say a word, Johnny had moved, and his mouth covered mine. Damn he could kiss. I started to melt into it, but realized I needed to end this. I pushed him away, and Chris spun me to him. His kiss was even hotter.

Fuck it. I guess a threesome is on the menu then.

The two of them had their hands and mouths all over me. Nothing was left undiscovered. We made out for a long ass time until I would've done anything they asked. I wanted relief so badly. They had me on my knees on the floor of the van at the short end of the seat. They stood outside the van fucking me from behind.

Soon they would take turns pounding my pussy while the other perched on the seat in front of my face and fucked my throat. I had never had two guys at once before and loved it. I only wished I could feel both of them violate my labyrinth at once. That would probably be more than I could handle.

Johnny was behind me plowing into me when Chris came in my mouth. There was little warning. His thrusting turned jerky, and he came right away after that. Usually, there's enough time to prepare, but not with him. I almost gagged.

"She's all yours," he said, buckling his belt. He left the van, and I could hear his footsteps cross the shop floor.

"Ready?" Johnny asked.

I thought he was asking if I was ready for him to cum. I nodded yes, preparing to turn around as soon as he pulled out to swallow his load.

He pulled out and rammed his cock straight into my ass. A scream escaped my lips. There was no preparation for that. He kept ramming his dick into my ass over and over. I gripped the van seat, squeezing as hard as I could with my eyes tightly pressed shut.

Johnny reached around and

rubbed my clit. To my surprise, and sheer horror, I came. The walls of my pussy convulsed, and my juices flowed down my inner thighs.

"I knew you were a dirty girl," he said.

His words insulted me, but they turned me on as well. I'd never thought of myself as dirty before, and I kind of liked it.

A few more thrusts, and I could feel his movements becoming jerky. He thrust into my ass one more time. It was his deepest drilling yet, and he spewed his cum into me.

I came into work Saturday morning regretting everything that happened the night before. I didn't regret the sex so much as I dreaded the new gossip that would be circulating. This had to stop. There could be no more evening hookups with the mechanics.

And there wouldn't be. That was guaranteed. I was surprised to see Mr. Rossi in the office when I walked in. Apparently, his daughter noticed a hickey on her husband's neck when he came home the night before. Johnny wasn't his son. He was his son-in-law.

So that's how I lost *that* job...

Chapter Seven

Dear Diary,

The interview at the Bridges Estate did not go well at all. I don't know what I'm going to do now. The semester is almost over, but I had to max out both my credit cards to make the tuition payments. If I don't find, and keep, a job soon, I won't be able to enroll next semester. There won't be any money to pay for it.

Luckily, I have close to a month before the semester begins, but who hires over the holidays? No one. Also, who wants to hire someone with my job history?

Definitely no one.

I don't know what's wrong with me. I never used to whore around like this. It's like I got a little independence combined with anger at my folks for fucking me over on the college savings that I'd always been told was there for me, and I started fucking anything with a heartbeat. If I could keep my clothes on until after I went home from my shift, I'd still have a job. Maybe.

There was no way I could tell any of this to Mr. Bridges. He's a strictly no nonsense type of guy. The interview for the nanny position made me feel like I was in a convent school and was in trouble for wearing my dress a half inch too short. It seemed like he was judging me the entire time, and it was obvious he was not happy with what he saw sitting across from him.

He asked if I had any experience with kids. I babysat in high school sometimes. That was my main experience with children. There were some young cousins in the family, but I only saw them at holidays and special occasions. All the adults would scramble for time with the babies, so I barely did anything more than a quick wave. I didn't tell him that though. I stuck to my babysitting history and tried to make it sound more impressive than it actually was.

It doesn't look like it made a

difference. Every time he looked at me, his eyes would squint, and he'd scrunch up his nose. Then the big question came. He brought up my work history. I've had three jobs, and the longest I've worked at any of them was three weeks. It doesn't look good. Anyone could see that, and I'd be a fool to try and pretend otherwise. I just couldn't tell him the truth. It was tempting though. A couple times when he looked my way, I thought I saw his eyes glance at my chest before giving me a disapproving look. It made me want to undo the top button or two on my blouse, but I really didn't think it would be in my favor to do that at this intcrview.

'Oh, it's because I've turned into

a slut who will fuck any man who smiles at me. It wouldn't be a problem except some of the men are married, some had their children walk in on us, and all of it occurred at work, on the clock. There were even security cameras involved once.'

That won't make me sound like the best choice to have around your child. Instead, I lied and claimed the reason I didn't work out anywhere was because I had a difficult time mastering the software for the jobs. Although I was more truthful about the deli. I admitted my ex-boyfriend was a shift manager there, and working alongside him didn't work out.

He explained he needed

someone days during the week. There would be no scheduling around my classes. The nanny had to be here with his daughter while he was at work. Once the spring semester starts, I could take evening and online classes, but until then, I needed to finish out my current schedule. That made him scowl. There were still two weeks left in the semester. I guess he wants someone to start right away.

The interview ended with the usual line about having more interviews scheduled, and he'd let me know. He said he'd call and let me know one way or the other by Friday. Employers say that, but they never follow through. I may only have had three jobs, but I've been to countless interviews. I've learned when employers say they'll let you know, it means the position is going to someone else.

I left the estate knowing I wouldn't get a call and began applying for all the jobs listed. I even applied at places who weren't advertising when I got to the end of the want ads. Between my work history and the time of the year, I knew it was unlikely to find anything, but I had to try. At the end of each week, I'd look at the calendar and figure out again what was the last day I could begin a job and still be able to pay my first tuition installment. That didn't even take into consideration my credit card payments. It became more and more overwhelming, and I felt completely screwed, only not in the good way.

The semester ended then the holidays came and went, first Christmas then the New Year. I had less than three weeks till the spring semester began. If I didn't start working immediately, I'd have to drop my classes.

I got called for another interview, and I went out of desperation. It wasn't a job I wanted at all. Things went well. I was given a quick tour of the building and was introduced to some of the employees. At the end, I was offered the job, and I accepted. It wasn't like I had much choice. I was given a start date which was that coming Monday and checked on paydays which were bi-weekly. As luck would have it, my first paycheck would be issued the day before my next tuition payment was due.

When I left, I sat in the parking lot for a long time. I parked facing away from the place, so no one could really see me. Even if they knew it was me out in that car, they might just think I was on the phone. They wouldn't be able to see the tears that streamed easily down my face. This is what my life had become.

It wasn't like I was born with a silver spoon in my mouth. I went without a lot growing up. There wasn't money for me to have everything I wanted, but part of the reason for that was because my parents were putting money into my college fund every paycheck. On the other hand, I didn't have to work. School was my job. I heard my parents say it so many times. They gave me an allowance to cover anything fun I wanted to do or buy, but they still took care of the big things like specific shoes needed for cheerleading. Somehow I went from having a home where I was provided for and college was a given to being the new fry girl at a fast food chain in less than six months. I could always just fuck some rando in the walk in cooler and get fired in a couple weeks if I really hated it.

While I was sitting in my car wallowing in my self-pity, my phone rang. I didn't recognize the number and almost didn't answer it. The only reason I finally did was because it might be someone calling for an interview off the minimum of a hundred applications I had filled out last month. Imagine my surprise to learn it was Mr. Bridges on the other end of the line.

It was surreal to hear him offer me the nanny position. The call was weeks later than he had said in the interview. I would have to start on Monday. There could be no way around that, and he needed me to come by today for a tour, paperwork, and to get all the important crap out of the way because he wouldn't be able to do it any other time. No problem. I could be right there.

I learned a little more about the job and about Mr. Bridges. There was only his one child who was ten months old. It sounded easy enough. I would only be responsible for his daughter Zoe and her nursery. I was welcome to use any room of the house during the day except for the bedrooms so long as I cleaned up after myself.

My room was in the finished basement. It was a mini-suite. There was a living room, complete with a television hooked up with cable, a small kitchenette, and a private bathroom off my bedroom.

My meals were my responsibility. Aside from feeding the baby, I didn't prepare food for the house or eat with him.

At the top of the basement stairs, there was a hallway with a number of rooms off it including the main living room. At the end of the hallway was the garage. This was the entrance I was to use. I'd be given the code to the garage door even though I had to park in the lane. Once in the garage, I'd use that door to enter the house, and I would be given the alarm code as well. I was to come and go down this hallway, and I was to keep as scarce as possible when I wasn't on the clock. Mr. Bridges often had visitors, and the nanny wasn't someone he wanted to be a permanent topic of conversation because she kept walking past them. If I was out late, I needed to be quiet as a mouse when coming home to not wake him or his daughter. I wasn't sure how that'd be possible seeing as how their rooms were upstairs.

Then he told me something I wish he'd kept to himself. I wasn't his first choice. The nanny he hired had been fired for sneaking men into her room. One of those men came upstairs in nothing but his boxers looking for milk when Mr. Bridges parents were visiting.

But not only was I not his first choice, I wasn't even his second. He began calling his second choice, then third and so on from the round of interviews last month. I was the first one to still be available. "The rest had found jobs," he said, sounding like it was another judgement he was passing on me.

He was taking out another ad and would be conducting more interviews to have options in case I didn't work out. The way he said it made it sound like he didn't expect me to last long. I left his home and went home to do the math. Three weeks. If I worked three weeks, I could make the first tuition payment and make my credit card payments with a little leftover. If I worked five weeks, I could make two payments and pay off one credit card. That was my goal. Five weeks, and I'd continue to look for a different job because I could tell Mr. Bridges didn't have long term plans for me.

Chapter Eight

Dear Diary,

Okay. New, more realistic goals. Five weeks isn't going to happen. I'm still holding out hope for three, but I have a feeling I won't make it to the end of week one.

I moved in last weekend. That went fine. Sort of. Mr. Bridges gave me a quick tour of the house. Well, he showed me the rooms I was allowed to use. That was basically the full extent of the tour. This is the family room, kitchen, etc. He explained that he expected anything needing cleaned up to be done during my regular shift as there would be no overtime. The rest of the rooms he didn't even say what they were. We just passed a lot of closed doors while he barked that they were off limits.

He left for a while shortly after I began unloading my car. It made it easier for me because I have a feeling he would've had an opinion about how much, or how little, I was bringing with me. He has a very concrete opinion about everything and is never afraid to share it.

After I made the last trip, I realized I was stuck. I hadn't been given any of the alarm codes yet. If I needed to, I could leave and lock thc door bchind me because I did at least have a key. It wouldn't be as secure without the alarm, and Mr. Bridges struck me as the type of person who would be irate to learn the alarm wasn't enabled.

There wasn't much I needed to do. I had planned on spending the evening unpacking and arranging everything I brought with me. That was after I went to the store to stock my little kitchen. I didn't want to leave a loaded car in the parking lot while I shopped especially with my laptop and other devices in there. It didn't seem like a big deal to unload then hit the grocery store. I just didn't expect Mr. Bridges to leave so suddenly.

On one of my trips to my car, I noticed his SUV was no longer in the garage. It still wasn't there when I had finished. He'd given me his cell phone number in case I needed to get ahold of him, and I knew it'd look bad messaging him so soon. I decided to wait.

I started unpacking instead. It was mostly clothes. I got all of that put away then moved on to my toiletries and make up. The bedroom and bathroom were done. There wasn't much left, but I decided to creep upstairs to see if he was home. I softly made my way down the hall as quietly as possible, but I didn't see anyone. I opened the door to the garage, and his SUV was still gone.

By now, my stomach was beginning to tell me that I needed to get to the store, and I needed to get there now. But what was I supposed to do? I knew if I waited, he'd be gone for hours. If I left, he'd get home five minutes after I pulled away. He'd be pissed over the house not being locked up properly and probably fire me on the spot. I'd have to repack everything I just got done putting away.

Instead, I went back to the basement and finished what little I had left to unpack in the hopes he'd be back before I finished. It was mainly kitchen stuff. There were a few dishes and pans that my parents could spare or had been donated for me by their friends. It wasn't much at all, but I didn't need to be able to make a Thanksgiving feast. I only needed to have the ability to make a few fast things for myself. Other than that, I only had my school supplies, electronics, and a few odds and ends like a couple small photos in frames to make the place feel homey.

I think it took seven and a half minutes once I went back downstairs. Without thinking, I broke down one of the boxes to put in the recycle bin. As soon as I did it, I regretted it. I'd be needing them again soon I was sure. I took it and the other boxes and put them in the closet near the bottom of the stairs. It contained a vacuum and hanging bar. It was meant for things like coats or other rarely used items, but I made room for the boxes instead.

There was still no sign of Mr. Bridges. *'Fuck it,'* I thought. *'I'm texting him.'*

"Hey, I've got everything settled. I guess all that's left is getting the codes for the house."

I tried to make it sound as innocent as possible. I didn't want to directly ask him because I get the feeling that anything could be enough to subject me to immediate termination. The man was a total dick. It didn't take long to get a reply.

"Yes, I'm aware."

Well, good to know asshole. Meanwhile your new nanny is going to starve because you didn't think to give her this information before you left her alone on her fucking day off.

"I don't feel comfortable giving that information over the phone. I'll give you the codes when I get back from supper with my parents."

Supper? Must be fucking nice. I checked the time, and it was 5:30. Even if they were early eaters, I should be able to make it to the store and back before he got home. I was too hungry to care. I would care if I got fired, of course. At least I was smart enough to push my start date at the fast food joint back a week, so if this went up in flames quick, I had a fall back. It was a Plan B I didn't want to have to use. Right then, the only thing I cared about was getting food in my system, and I was too broke to order out.

I did have a key to the door at least. It was better than nothing. I locked it behind me, leaving the garage door open and went to the nearest store. It was almost a twenty minute drive one way which started to worry me.

I made it through the aisles as quickly as I could. Ramen noodles, pop tarts and dry cereal, some juice packets, and a few other items were all I could afford. It was the last of my cash, but it'd last me till at least the end of the week. I'd have to figure out what I'd do the following week before I got paid.

Once I was back in my car, I sped like the devil back to Mr.

Bridges' house. I held my breath the entire way up the quarter mile drive to the front of the house, but to my sheer luck, his SUV was still gone. That's when it occurred to me he probably has a surveillance system. Oh, well. Done was done.

I brought my groceries down stairs and put them away. There certainly wasn't much. I could probably stretch the Ramen two weeks if I was careful. I'd bought several cases. It looked like I was going on a completely unnecessary crash diet until payday.

After I ate, I was a nervous wreck while waiting on Mr. Bridges to get home. I couldn't sit still. I tried to find something to watch, but nothing kept my attention long.

I kept hopping up and pacing the floor, wondering if I should go upstairs and check or not. I did a few times, but it became harder and harder to build up my nerve. It was a real catch twenty-two. I had to go into the main floor of the house to come and go, but I was also supposed to make my presence as scarce as possible during my time off. It was a set up for the nanny to fail if you ask me.

Finally, I gave up. It was almost nine o'clock. He'd leave for work in a little over ten hours. I took a long shower in case I overslept in the morning, brushed out my long brunette hair and pulled it back. I put on a nightie and wrapped myself in a matching short robe thinking I'd head to bed and get the codes in the morning.

Then I'd remembered I'd have nothing to drink but water tomorrow, so I decided to go into the kitchen. I was going to make a pitcher of juice, so it'd have time to chill in the fridge overnight. I opened my bedroom door, and there was Mr. Bridges. He was about three feet away checking out the little touches of decor I added to the living room. I gasped loudly. He scared the living shit out of me.

"I apologize," he said when he saw me. "I didn't mean to startle you. I put Zoe to bed and came downstairs to give you the codes."

'You could've fucking sent a text to let me know you were home,' I

thought.

"I tried texting you, but you didn't respond.

And he had sent a single text saying he was home and to come to the kitchen for the codes. I saw it after he left, but I hadn't checked my phone since my shower.

"I wasn't sure if you were asleep or maybe caught up in a movie," he continued, motioning to the television. "Anyway, I wrote them down for you." Mr. Bridges picked up a piece of paper off the coffee table. "The codes for the garage and the alarm system are here as well as instructions. It's pretty straight forward. I'd hate for you to have to leave with the house being unsecured."

Something about the way he said those words told me he knew I left earlier. A man like him would not only have security cameras, but would be able to access them from his phone as well.

He looked me over, and I pulled my robe tighter around me feeling naked even though I knew I was completely covered. There was something about the way his eyes traveled my body that told me he wanted to see more. Mr. Bridges was over twice my age. I'd been with some older guys the last six months, but that was ridiculous.

Something broke him out of his trance. "Goodnight, Sierra," he said. "See you in the morning."

I walked over to the paper as he

left. The instructions were straight forward like he said. "Wait," I said without thinking.

He stopped about halfway up the stairs and turned back to me.

I suddenly felt like a little child about to ask for something I know I'm not supposed to have. "What about the Wi-Fi password?" I asked.

"Wi-Fi?" he repeated. "Don't you have a cell phone?"

"Yes," I told him. "But for my laptop," I said, pointing to the desk in the corner of the living room. "For school."

Mr. Bridges straightened up. "You live here for free and even have the ability to control the temperature down here," he said, pointing to the thermostat. "The television has cable, and I programmed all of my streaming services into it. I think that's enough. Next you'll be asking to help yourself to what's in my kitchen. Use your hot spot," he said before walking up the rest of the stairs.

What an ass! Not everyone has unlimited data on their phones. That would be me. I'm not everyone.

My future would be spent at the college library during all my free time. I don't mind really because it's not like I have much of a social life. It's just the point. I'll have to spend a lot of extra gas money going back and forth now. What's the point of having online classes if I still have to drive to the campus for them?

He is so infuriating! I stood there shocked for a couple moments after he left before heading to bed pissed off at the whole situation. And I completely forgot to make juice for the morning.

Chapter Nine

Dear Diary,

The three week mini goal is definitely in sight. In fact, I'd make a prediction about the five week goal, but I'm afraid I'd jinx myself into joblessness tonight. This is the end of my first two weeks. It's gone off without a hitch.

Zoe just turned eleven months and is obviously easy to care for at that age. I meet Mr. Bridges in the kitchen around 7:30. He leaves shortly after that, but it depends on the day. His daughter is already in the high chair, dressed for the day, and eating whatever breakfast he chose for her.

He's very hands on when it comes to parenting. I'll give him that. Her lunch and snacks are always set out on the counter, so I don't have to think about it. She takes a nap in the morning and one in the afternoon. I don't do a whole lot for the money I earn, but there is a catch.

Mr. Bridges is a big wig at an insurance company in the city. It's the same one Mr. Scott represented as an agent. Sometimes he travels for business. That's where the real nanny work comes in for me. I will be paid a little extra when he's out of town, but not a lot since I'm already making cake money. We discussed what happens when I have evening classes while he's gone. There's a list of babysitters in his office that he uses for rare occasions. They've all been approved by him. I'm welcome to use any of them, but it's at my own personal expense.

As much as it sucks, I guess it's better than no job.

I do have to wonder. If he leaves town for a week, will he put seven days' worth of food for Zoe on the counter?

Anyway, he comes home and cooks dinner for the two of them. By cooks, I mean he usually orders out or brings take out home with him. There are times when he whips up something in the kitchen. He plays with her and bathes her before bed. I'm not around for it most of the time, but I've seen him on the floor with her crawling around when I was headed to and from the library for school.

One night, I came through as Zoe climbed all over him. They were both laughing so hard. I watched them for a couple minutes because he was too wrapped up in his daughter to pay me any attention, but I didn't want to risk hanging around for too long.

It made me remember a conversation I had with my mom a very long time ago. I asked her what attracted her to dad. My dad was middle aged, had a bit of a belly, and was balding. I couldn't say it outright, but I had no idea what my mom saw in him, how they got together. She was an exquisite beauty, and he looked like he was just lucky to be at the party.

My mom told me that what attracts you to someone changes as your life changes. In high school, you're attracted to what will upset your parents the most. I had to laugh at that. In college, it's looks, but also big ideas for the future and wanting to change the world. Once you're marriage minded, you're attracted to how the person is as a partner and would be as a parent to your child.

Remembering that made me think Mr. Bridges must be an extraordinarily attractive man. Ugh. Where did that thought come from? I was far from becoming a mom, and Mr. Bridges was far from attractive in any other sense of the word.

So anyway like I said, I got my first paycheck today. After work, I filled my car with gas. *'My car.'* It's my mom's old car because my parents felt bad about siphoning my college fund. Better than no car. Then I drove to the campus just before the main office closed. Luckily, they keep evening hours. I paid the first tuition payment for classes that would begin on Monday. I saved back enough money to fill my tank again because I knew I'd need it then I spent the rest of it on groceries. More ramen, pop tarts, and I splurged and bought a few pieces of fruit. They'd have to double as a dessert. I brought everything back to my basement apartment and put it away, pulling out a package of Ramen for dinner when a voice behind me scared the crap out of me again.

There had to be some way for him to let me know he was on his way downstairs. I definitely could never leave my bedroom naked to grab something real quick.

"Sorry for startling you. Again," he laughed. "I just want to make sure the deposit went through okay. Sometimes there's a hang up with the first payment."

"No, I got it," I said smiling. "Thank you."

Mr. Bridges looked at the package of Ramen in my hand and pursed his lips together. "I thought you went to the store," he said.

I wasn't sure if it was a comment or a question. "I did." I opened the cabinet to show him the four cases of Ramen I bought earlier. "There wasn't much left after tuition. Next week will be better," I added, having no clue why I felt the need to make him feel better about my food situation.

He nodded and headed to the stairs. Putting his hand on the rail, he paused. "I'm ordering out pizza. Would you like to join us?"

I wanted to. I really did, but I didn't want to be a pity case either. Before I could say no, he answered for me.

"Of course, you'll join us. You can come on up, or I can text you when it arrives."

With that, he left. I still wanted to say no, but my abdomen was presenting a strong argument in favor of pizza. I put the pan and the package of noodles away and headed up the stairs.

Mr. Bridges was in the living room with Zoe. I could tell she had already ate. It made me realize he ordered pizza on account of me. It was a nice gesture, and I will be appreciative is what I told myself.

Surprisingly, I had a pretty good night. It was the first real meal I had ate in weeks. I enjoyed playing with Zoe and watching him act like a regular guy, a good dad, instead of the asshole I normally had the displeasure of being around. At one point, he even told me to call him Nick. I repeated his name to him to be polite, but it felt foreign rolling off my tongue. Then to my horror, I had the thought that he really wasn't that bad looking of a guy.

No, Sierra. No! Do not go there. I need that like I need a hole in the head.

He took Zoe up for her bath, and I cleaned up from dinner, putting everything away. It was the least I could do to thank him for the meal. He was still upstairs when I went back to my room and changed into my nightie.

I found a movie to watch and settled in with the glass of the pop I'd brought down with me. He had told me I could have the rest of the two liter. While the opening credits started to roll, I reached for my phone to silence it. This movie was supposed to be extremely scary, and I didn't need a phone notification at the wrong time scaring the wits out of me, causing me to scream like a little girl. It wasn't on the end table.

I paused the movie and checked around the floor in case it fell. I reached my hand down along the cushions of my chair. It wasn't in the kitchen either. I must have left it upstairs. I put on my robe and headed up to fetch it.

As I walked down the hall, I thought I heard my name. I paused to see if he was talking about me whether to himself or perhaps on a phone call. Either way I was curious what he had to say. After another minute, I heard my name again. "Sierra." That was it. Weird.

I continued toward the family room, and as it came into view, I saw him. Mr. Bridges was sitting on the couch with a pair of sweats around his ankles. He no longer had a shirt on, and I could see his tan, muscular chest with a small trail of hair leading down to the biggest cock I'd ever laid my eyes on. It was massive. It would take both my hands to stroke it.

I can't believe I even thought

that! But it would. It was too large. It wouldn't fit anywhere. I probably couldn't even fit my mouth around the tip. Where were these thoughts coming from?!

As I stood there caught in surprise and growing curiosity, I heard him say my name again. "Sierra," he moaned.

He was jacking off while thinking about me. Holy shit!

His eyes were closed, and his head rested on the back of the couch facing up toward the ceiling. "I've wanted to fuck you till you can't walk for a month since the moment we met at your interview. God, your pussy is so tight. I'm going to cum."

He shot his load at that

moment, and it sprayed halfway across the room. I've never seen so much jizz come out of a man at one time.

I made my way quickly down the hall to the basement before he could realize he had an audience. I didn't realize how turned on it made me until I felt the wetness in my panties and felt my legs shaking as they tried to carry me to my room. I had no idea he felt that way about me.

New goal. Fuck the boss. Literally.

Chapter Ten

Dear Diary,

First, I made it through week five. It was going pretty well to be honest. The only thing that would have made it better would be the Wi-Fi password. Well that and Nick's massive member plowing into my pussy until it was wrecked.

One thing at a time though. I was dressing a little sexier. I mean ever so slight changes. It wasn't something I wanted to do drastically, so I've slowly decreased the length of my skirts and increased the tightness of my tops. If he's noticed, he hasn't said anything. It also means he doesn't necessarily disapprove.

And I've made myself more visible. I started making my trips to campus at times when I knew it would be likely for him to be downstairs. I was supposed to be as out of sight as possible during my off hours. That was no longer being followed. Instead, I made sure to be seen as I came and went. I was quiet and respectful, but he could definitely see me in my "street" clothes so to speak. Those outfits were much more revealing than what I wore during my work hours.

He never said a word to me about it. Nothing about how much I was seen, and nothing about my taste in clothing. I felt his eyes on me all the time. It made me hot knowing how much he wanted me. I don't think I've ever felt so desired. Yeah, other men had looked at me lustfully in the past, and sometimes it turned me on. There was something about Nick specifically that really drove it home between my legs. It made my clit throb with my heartbeat and my panties instantly wet. It had to be the memory of his hard shaft. I wanted to feel him tear me apart and was afraid of it too. That's what made me so damn susceptible to him.

Mr. Bridges, I mean Nick, was always a gentleman around me. Sure there were times when I knew he was checking me out. I'd catch him staring at my ass or my rack. Each time he'd get this disgusted look on his face and act all moral and proper again. I didn't understand it. The man masturbated while thinking about me, but found my cleavage repulsive. What gives?

I had set up multiple opportunities for us to accidentally come together in something illicit. He never took the bait. No matter how many times I tried, nothing worked. It was getting frustrating. I had one more ace up my sleeve. If it didn't work, I didn't think anything would. This was it. The game was on the line.

One night I prepared everything

in my basement suite. I waited until after Zoe would be asleep in her crib, and Nick would be wandering the house with the baby monitor in his hand. I set the mood with some music and candlelight. I put on my sexiest nightie. Now, I just needed him to do another surprise visit to my rooms.

I took out the only two pans I owned. One was a baking sheet, and the other was a sauce pan. I banged them together a couple times then dropped them on top of each other on the tile floor. It was loud enough to make my ears ring. I could only hope Nick would hear it, that he was close enough to the basement to hear it.

After making a ruckus, I put

the pans away. I could hear the footsteps running down the stairs as I did. I smiled, but had to stifle it. He couldn't know it was planned.

I left the kitchen for my living room not looking in the direction of the stairs. From the corner of my eye, I could see Nick standing at the base of them. His mouth hung open, and he was taking in all of me. I bent over in front of the television, grabbing a movie from the shelf below it. When I did, I angled my ass to give Nick a clear enough view to notice I wasn't wearing panties.

Then I turned quickly and feigned surprise to see him standing there. It was a delicate balance. I needed him to see enough to want to stay, but I couldn't take so long that he had a chance to come to his senses and sneak back upstairs.

"I'm so sorry," he said. "I didn't mean to..." he looked around, trying to find the words. "I didn't mean to barge in on you. I thought I heard something."

"Oh," I smiled. "I dropped the pans when I put away the dishes. I didn't realize it was so loud," I said, walking toward him.

I could tell the close proximity of me dressed in next to nothing was making him nervous. He opened and shut his mouth several times then he shifted his weight back and forth. Do or die. They say you only live once. I was going to fuck Nick tonight, or I was going to get fired trying.

"Since you're here," I began, taking another step in his direction. There were a few mere inches left between us. "There's something I was hoping you could help me with."

"Wh-what's that?" he asked. He cleared his throat after barely managing to get the question out.

I grabbed the hem of my nightie and lifted it off over my head. "This," I stated plainly.

Nick's eyes blinked several times. His gaze would divert to my body then he'd snap his eyes back to mine, but it wouldn't last long till they wandered again. "Um, Sierra," he said. "I –I..."

"Do you like what you see?" I asked, placing my hand on his bare chest. I loved how he only wore a pair of sweats around the house at night. It made his body so much more accessible.

"Sierra," he said again. His voice was more controlled.

"Because I really like what I see." I leaned in to kiss him, but he grabbed my arms and pushed me away.

'Damn,' I thought. *'I completely misjudged this. I'll be packed and moved out before bedtime.'*

I stared at the floor waiting for him to reprimand me. Waiting for him to yell. Waiting for him to tell me I'm fired. Waiting for him to say anything. He never did.

When I looked back up, he was staring at me. "I'm not telling you no," he explained. "I want to know you're sure."

A grin broke over my face. "I'm sure."

He looked at me again carefully. His eyes searching my face for any sign if I was telling the truth. He must've liked what he saw because he pulled me close and wrapped his arms around me. "Oh, Sierra. I've wanted you from day one. That's why I refused to offer you the job until I had no choice. I didn't trust myself not to make a move."

He pulled back and tilted his head. "How cliché? Fucking the nanny? I get angry every time I catch myself admiring your body and have to scold myself."

'So that's what those disgusted looks were about,' I realized.

Nick took my hand and led me to my bedroom. He walked me to the bed and pulled his sweatpants off to reveal that enormous cock I'd been fantasizing about since the moment I watched him pleasure himself. I couldn't help but stare.

He turned my words around on me. "Do you like what you see?" he asked.

I licked my lips. "I don't know how this is gonna work. You're not gonna fit inside me anywhere."

"You'd be surprised," he said, laying me back on the bed.

And surprised I was. Even more

shocking than how I managed to fit all eight inches of his massive shaft inside my tight pussy was the fact I was able to keep a job after having sex at work. I guess having a fulfilled boss is what makes the difference.

Coming Soon

Stay tuned for more of the Nanny Diaries and Family Secrets series by Darling Coxx! The second installment of the Family Secrets series is expected December 1, 2021!

More by Darling Coxx

Nanny Diaries #1

Lacey Moore bit off more than she could swallow when she took the position at the Wyndham estate.

What was supposed to be the perfect job accompanied by great hours, pay and perks like living rent free in the guest house soon turned out to be more than she had could have ever imagined. The main duties of her job included making sure the entire staff stayed satisfied, and it was a job she intended on doing well.

Nanny Diaries #2

Vicki Sweet didn't know what she was walking into when she took the job as nanny for the Rayburn's. Soon she found herself loaded with maid duties as well as chasing after the children while Aidan worked and ignored all of his wife's illicit activities. Tori Rayburn needed to be put in her place, and Vicki was just the woman for the job. Chasing after Tori's affairs, Vicki began stealing them away one by one, but her eye remained on the ultimate prize. Vicki would have her saucy way with Aidan before her job ended, and once she set her mind on something, she always got what she wanted.

Nanny Diaries #3

Mindy Cummings didn't except anything from Mark Jacobs expect a deccnt paying part time nanny job that worked well with her college schedule. The apartment over the garage for her own private affairs was an added bonus. She soon learned how little she knew about the man she'd been babysitting for since she was a teen. It wouldn't take long to realize that his touch was the one thing she needed more than anything. Fantasy after fantasy, he filled her thoughts. His face was who she envisioned no matter who she was with. The one thing she didn't expect was for fantasy to become reality.

Family Secrets: Lexi's Education

Lexi had lived a sheltered life thanks to her step-dad. He was a good man, a good, muscular, handsome, type of man. One thing he made sure of was that no one took advantage of his gorgeous step-daughter. Soon she'd be off to college in another state where she'd be at the mercy of the boys she met on campus. She needed a different type of education, a sexual education, and her step-dad was the right man for the job.

About the Author

Darling Coxx is a seasoned writer who has been featured in many major publications under her given name. Taking a break from interviews and personal experience pieces, she is trying her hand at short novellas in the same genre she's been working in for most of her life.

Her adult entertainment career began while working as the manager of an adult store. It is her favorite position of any she's held, before or since. It was there where she made the contacts that allowed her to venture into the world of adult entertainment both in her own writing as well as producing a few pieces of her own.

Please feel free to reach out to her at DarlingCoxx@gmail.com. Follow her on Instagram @DarlingCoxx to stay updated on future publications. And don't forget to subscribe to her OnlyFans account @DarlingCoxx.